# Buffy's Orange Leash

Stephen Golder
and
Lise Memling

Illustrated by Marcy Ramsey

Kendall Green Publications     Gallaudet University Press     Washington, D.C.

Kendall Green Publications
An imprint of Gallaudet University Press
Washington, DC 20002

Printed in the United States of America

Library of Congress Cataloging-in-Publication Data
Golder, Stephen, 1948-
    Buffy's orange leash/Stephen Golder and Lise Memling.
        p.   cm.
    Summary: Describes how a particular hearing ear dog was selected
and trained and how he helps his deaf owners.
    ISBN 0-930323-42-4
    1. Hearing ear dogs—Juvenile literature. [1. Hearing ear dogs.
2. Dogs—Training.] I. Memling, Lise, 1949-    . II. Title.
HV2509.G65 1988
636.7'088—dc19                                                88-21293
                                                                  CIP
                                                                  AC

Reinforced binding

Gallaudet University is an equal opportunity employer/educational institution.
Programs and services offered by Gallaudet University receive substantial
financial support from the U.S. Department of Education.

With many thanks to Carolyn Bird, Isabelle Conrad, Adele Polk, and Daisy, and the Red Acre Farm Hearing Dog Center. And to all Hearing Dog centers everywhere whatever the color of their dogs' leashes.

And, of course, for Joshua.

Buffy is a furry white dog who lives with the Johnson family.

Buffy lives with Mr. Johnson, Mrs. Johnson, and little Billy Johnson. The Johnsons are not ordinary people. Can you guess what makes the Johnson family a little bit different?

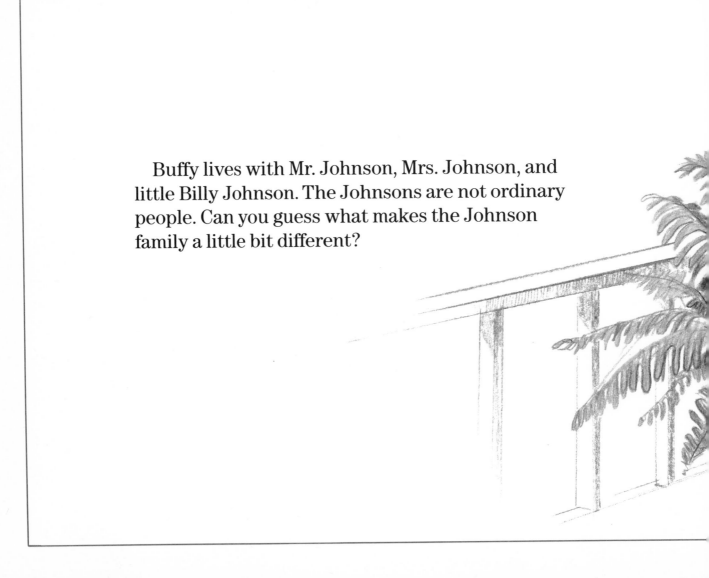

Mr. and Mrs. Johnson can't hear—they are deaf. They can't hear any sounds. They can't hear the telephone or the doorbell ringing, the kettle whistling, or Billy crying.

The Johnsons are not able to hear, but they certainly can talk. They use their hands to talk in sign language.

Come

Sit

Stay

Buffy is not an ordinary dog. He is a Hearing Dog. He uses his ears to help Mr. and Mrs. Johnson hear important sounds in their home.

Buffy also understands five signs that the Johnsons use when they talk to him.

**Heel**

**Down**

When Buffy was young, he lived in a kennel. One day, two people from the Red Acre Farm Hearing Dog Center visited the kennel. They looked at many different dogs. They chose Buffy to be a Hearing Dog. Why did they choose him? Buffy was friendly.

Buffy was smart. And Buffy liked to listen. He was more interested in listening than in looking or sniffing.

The Hearing Dog trainers took Buffy from the kennel. They brought him to Red Acre Farm Hearing Dog Center. Red Acre Farm is a school that teaches dogs to help deaf people.

The trainers taught Buffy how to listen for
certain sounds, like the doorbell and the telephone.

When Buffy finished school, his trainers gave him an orange leash and collar. All Hearing Dogs from Red Acre Farm wear an orange leash and collar.

The trainers also gave Mr. and Mrs. Johnson a card with Buffy's picture on it. This card tells everyone that Buffy is a Hearing Dog.

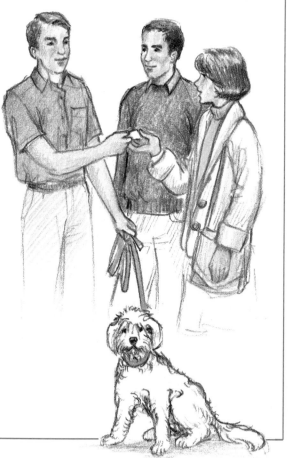

At school Buffy learned many ways to help the Johnson: When the telephone rings, Buffy runs over and touches th Johnsons and leads them to their telephone.

The Johnsons have a special telephone because they can't hear people talking. Their telephone looks like a typewriter. It is called a TDD. The TDD lets the Johnsons type their conversations over the telephone.

Buffy listens for many sounds. When he hears someone ring the doorbell or knock on the door, he touches the Johnsons and leads them to the door.

Buffy learned to wake up Mr. and Mrs. Johnson. When the alarm clock goes off in the morning, Buffy jumps up on the bed.

Buffy nudges the Johnsons until they wake up. Then they get up and give Billy his breakfast and get ready for work.

Buffy does other jobs, too. One of Buffy's other jobs is to listen for Billy.

When Billy cries or makes noise, Buffy runs over to Mr. or Mrs. Johnson. He leads one of them over to Billy.

Buffy's most important job is to warn the Johnsons when the smoke detector goes off. The Johnsons can't hear it, so they need Buffy to tell them when it beeps.

Buffy runs over and touches the Johnsons and then quickly drops to the floor when he hears the beep. That is how he tells them there is a fire.

The Johnsons love Buffy and pet
him all the time, especially right after he
helps them. When they pet Buffy, it helps
him to remember his hearing jobs. Buffy is
an important member of the Johnson family.

Buffy can go wherever the Johnsons go. He wears his bright orange leash and collar. The special leash and collar tell people that he is a Hearing Dog that helps deaf people.

Now you know what a Hearing Dog is. One day you may see Buffy
or another Hearing Dog helping a deaf person. Then, you can tell
your friends all about Buffy's orange leash.